USEFUL INFORMATION

LIQUID MEASURE

4 gills (gi.) = 1 pint (pt.)
2 pints = 1 quart (qt.)
4 quarts = 1 gallon (gal.) (231 cu. in.)
31½ gallons = 1 barrel (bbl.)
2 barrels = 1 hogshead (hhd.)
1 cubic foot of water = 7.48 gallons
1 cubic foot of water weighs approximately 62½ pounds.

CUBIC MEASURE

1728 cubic inches (cu. in.) = 1 cubic foot (cu. ft.)
27 cubic feet = 1 cubic yard (cu yd.)
16 cubic feet = 1 cord foot of wood
128 cubic feet or 8 cord feet = 1 cord of wood

NOTE:—A cord of wood is equivalent to a pile 8 feet long, 4 feet wide, and 4 feet high.

24¾ cubic feet = 1 perch (P.)

NOTE:—A perch of stone or brick is equivalent to a section 16½ feet long, 1½ feet wide, and 1 foot high. The unit is sometimes understood to mean 16½ cubic feet and sometimes 25 cubic feet.

40 cubic feet = 1 measurement ton, U. S. Shipping
42 cubic feet = 1 ton British Shipping
40 feet of round timber, or 50 feet of hewn timber = 1 ton or load

AVOIRDUPOIS WEIGHT

(Used in weighing all articles except drugs, gold, silver and precious stones)

27-11/32 grains (gr.) = 1 dram (dr.)
16 drams (437½ grs.) = 1 ounce (oz.)
16 ounces (7000 grs.) = 1 pound (lb.)
25 pounds = 1 quarter (qr.)
4 quarters or 100 pounds = 1 hundred-weight (cwt.)
2000 pounds or 20 hundredweight = 1 ton (T.)

NOTE:—The ton and hundredweight above given are those in common use in the United States.

2240 pounds = 1 long ton (L. T.)
13¼ cubic feet of air weighs = 1 pound

NOTE:—The grain has the same value in the Avoirdupois, Apothecaries' and Troy systems.

MISCELLANEOUS

12 units = 1 dozen
12 dozen = 1 gross
12 gross = 1 great gross
20 units = 1 score
4 inches = 1 hand
Diameter of circle x 3.1416 = circumference
Circumference of circle x .3183 = diameter
Diameter of circle squared x .7854 = area
Atmospheric pressure is 14.7 lbs. per square inch at sea level.

SQUARE MEASURE

144 square inches = 1 square foot (sq. ft.)
9 square feet = 1 square yard (sq. yd.)
30¼ square yards or 272¼ square feet = 1 square rod or 1 perch
40 square rods = 1 rood (R.)
160 square rods = 1 acre (A.)
640 acres = 1 square mile (sq. mi.)

A square having an area of 1 acre, measures 208.71 feet on each side.

1 township = 36 sections each 1 mile square
1 section = 640 acres
¼ section = ½ mile square or 160 acres
⅛ section = ½ mile long and ¼ mile wide or 80 acres
1 acre = 4840 square yards
1 acre = a lot 208.71 feet square

LINEAR MEASURE

1/12 inch = 1 line
12 inches = 1 foot (ft.)
3 feet = 1 yard (yd.)
5½ yards or 16½ feet = 1 rod (rd.) or pole
40 rods (660 feet) = 1 furlong (fur.)
320 rods (5280 feet or 8 furlongs) = 1 statute mile (m.)
3 miles = 1 league
6 feet = 1 fathom
120 fathoms = 1 cable-length
7⅓ cables = 1 statute mile
5280 feet = 1 statute mile
6080.2 feet = 1 geographical or nautical mile
1 geographical mile = 1.15155 statute mile
60 geographical miles = 1 degree longitude at equator
360 degrees = circumference of earth at equator

CIRCULAR MEASURE

60 seconds (") = 1 minute (')
60 minutes = 1 degree (°)
90 degrees = 1 quadrant
360 degrees = 1 circumference

A degree of the earth's surface on a meridian equals approximately 69 miles.

APOTHECARIES' FLUID MEASURE

60 minims = 1 fluid dram
8 fluid drams = 1 fluid ounce
16 fluid ounces = 1 pint
8 pints = 1 gallon

MULTIPLICATION TABLE

1	2	3	4	5	6	7	8	9	10	11	12
2	4	6	8	10	12	14	16	18	20	22	24
3	6	9	12	15	18	21	24	27	30	33	36
4	8	12	16	20	24	28	32	36	40	44	48
5	10	15	20	25	30	35	40	45	50	55	60
6	12	18	24	30	36	42	48	54	60	66	72
7	14	21	28	35	42	49	56	63	70	77	84
8	16	24	32	40	48	56	64	72	80	88	96
9	18	27	36	45	54	63	72	81	90	99	108
10	20	30	40	50	60	70	80	90	100	110	120
11	22	33	44	55	66	77	88	99	110	121	132
12	24	36	48	60	72	84	96	108	120	132	144

To My Big Brother and little Sister

Library of Congress Cataloging-in-Publication Data available.

ISBN 978-1-4521-8180-6

Manufactured in China.

MIX
Paper from responsible sources
FSC™ C104723
FSC
www.fsc.org

Design by Jay Marvel.
Typeset in Freight Text.
The illustrations in this book were rendered in watercolor, pencil, art from a few centuries ago, digital media, and a whole lot more.

Special thanks to the Rijksmuseum for use of their engravings and other art they generously entered into the public domain.

10 9 8 7 6 5 4 3 2 1

Chronicle Books LLC
680 Second Street
San Francisco, California 94107

Chronicle Books—we see things differently.
Become part of our community at www.chroniclekids.com.

THE MIDDLE KID

KID

BY STEVEN WEINBERG

chronicle books · san francisco

Table of Contents

Dear You,

This is a book about me. THE MIDDLE KID.

You might ask: "Hey, what is a middle kid?"

Well, a middle kid is:

-The one who gets blamed when your little sister is CRYING.

-The one who gets BEAT UP when your big brother is mad.

-Not the youngest. Not the oldest. SOMEWHERE IN THE MIDDLE.

Me.

Sometimes I hate it.

Sometimes I love it.

This book is a day in my life. GOOD LUCK!

Right in between,

THE MIDDLE KID

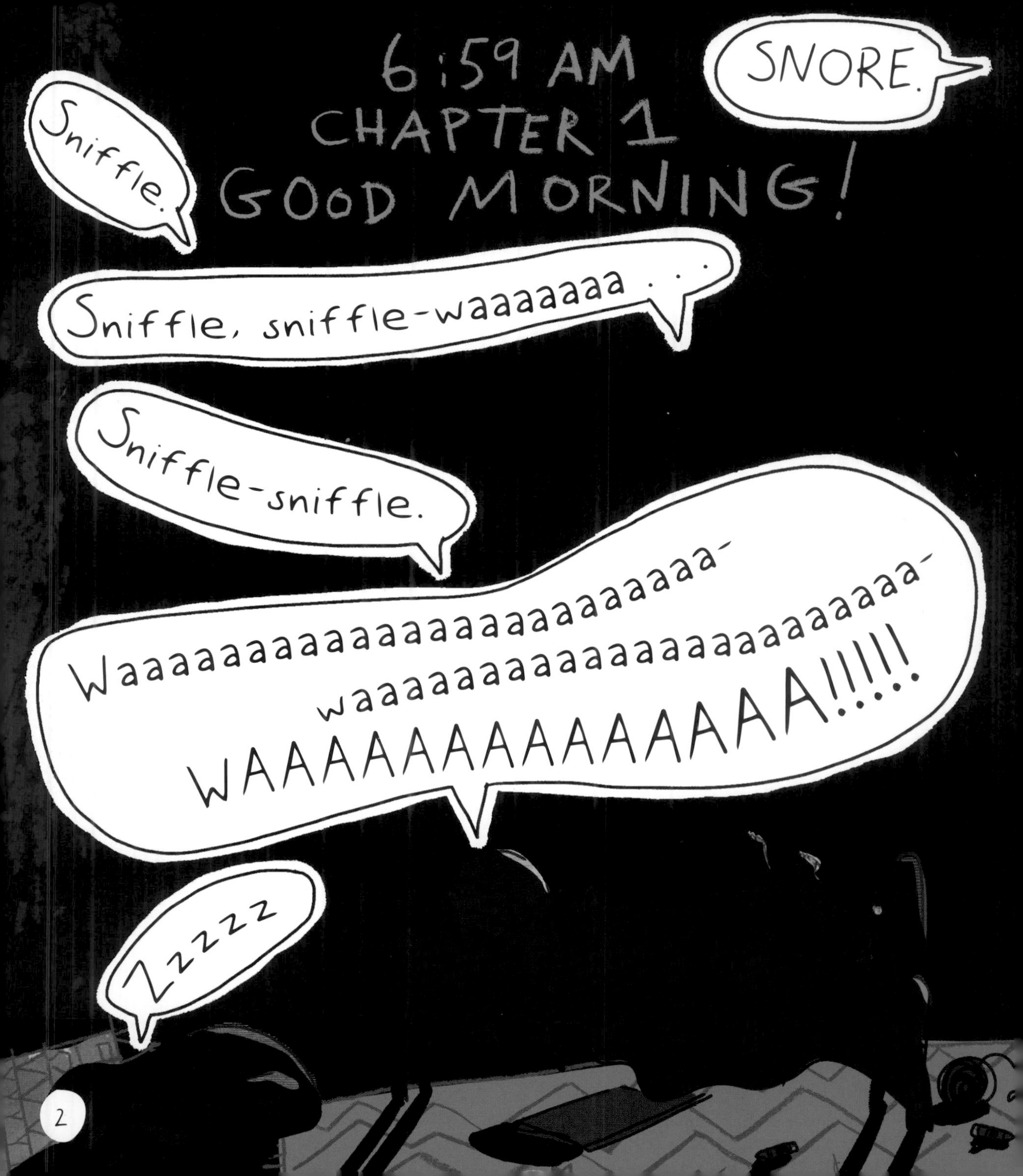

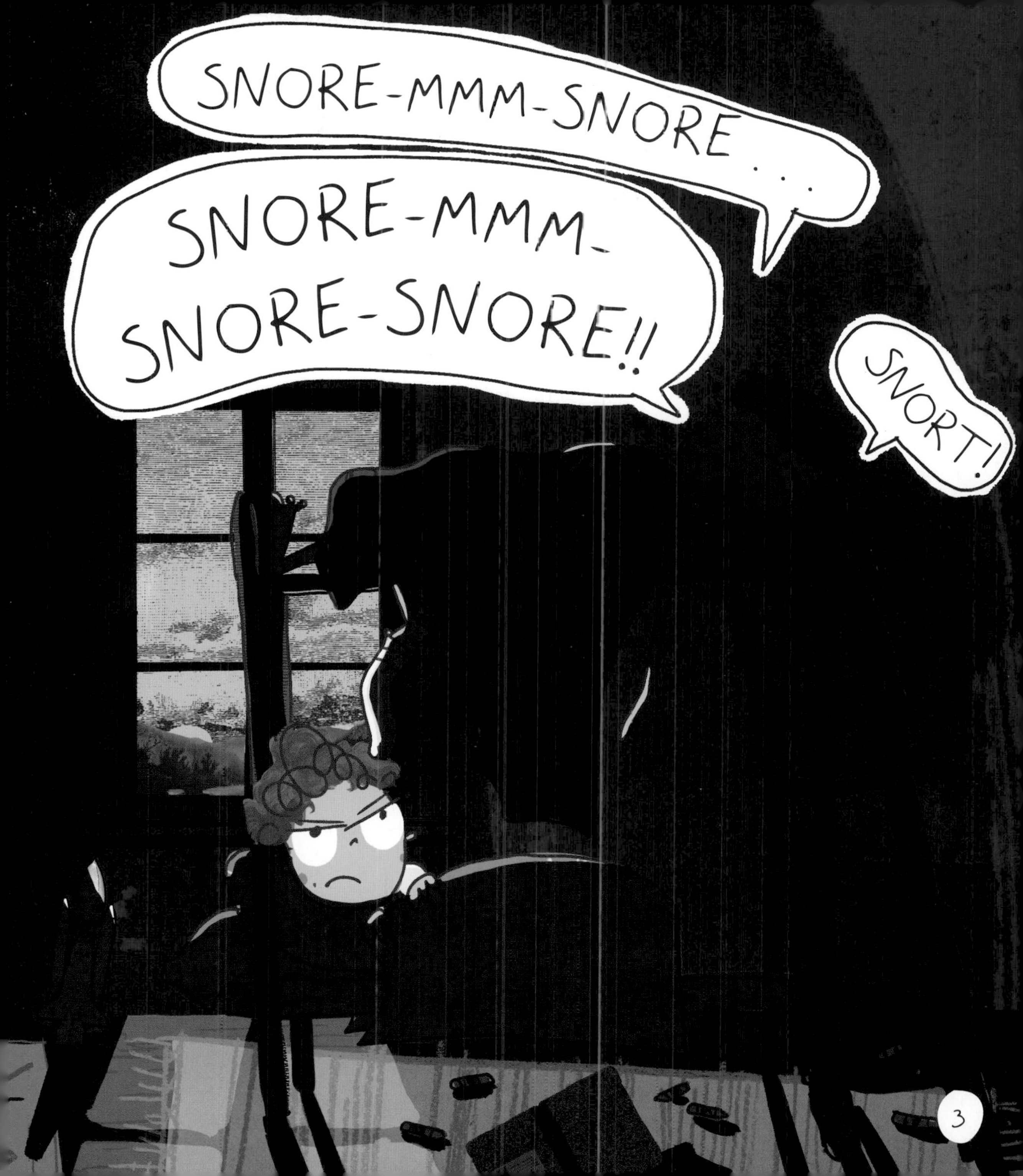
SNORE-MMM-SNORE . . .
SNORE-MMM-SNORE-SNORE!!
SNORT!

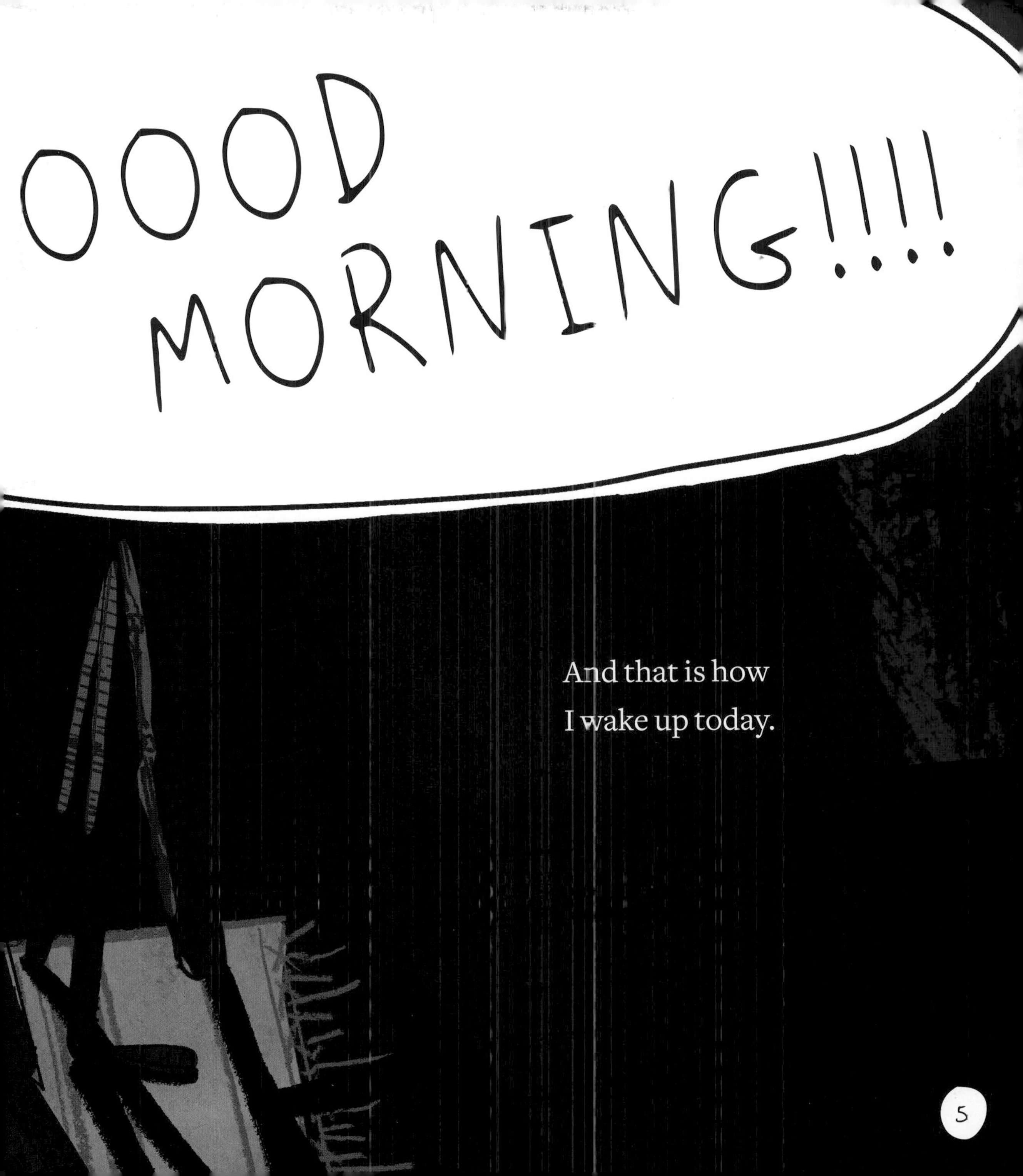

And that is how
I wake up today.

PASS THE OJ.
HEY! I SAID PASS THE OJ!

I am drawing.

I love drawing. Drawing is the only time
no one tells me I am too loud.

I am drawing a castle.

It has big towers, strong walls, and a moat with tigers. Castles need to be superstrong. They are always getting attacked.

See what I mean?

Attacked from both sides.

The life of a kid in the middle.

YOU GOTTA BE <u>TOUGH</u>

This morning, my big brother tells me, "You gotta be tough."

"I AM!" I yell.

"No," he says. "You are loud. Loud is not tough." I turn around. I have things to draw.

He grabs my shoulder and says, "I will teach you how to be tough. Because I am tough. And I have your back."

That might be the nicest thing he has ever told me.

Then he stops looking so nice.

He says, "Come with me."

I am not tough yet, so I do not say no.

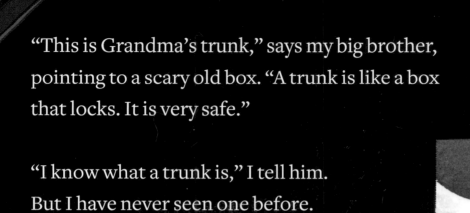

"This is Grandma's trunk," says my big brother, pointing to a scary old box. "A trunk is like a box that locks. It is very safe."

"I know what a trunk is," I tell him.
But I have never seen one before.

"Like I was saying," he says. "You are not tough. But you gotta be."

THIS TRUNK WILL MAKE YOU TOUGH.

MALI

Ελλάδα

But my big brother
isn't listening.

He's too busy being tough.

13

10:50 AM

CHAPTER 4
BUNGEE JUMPING

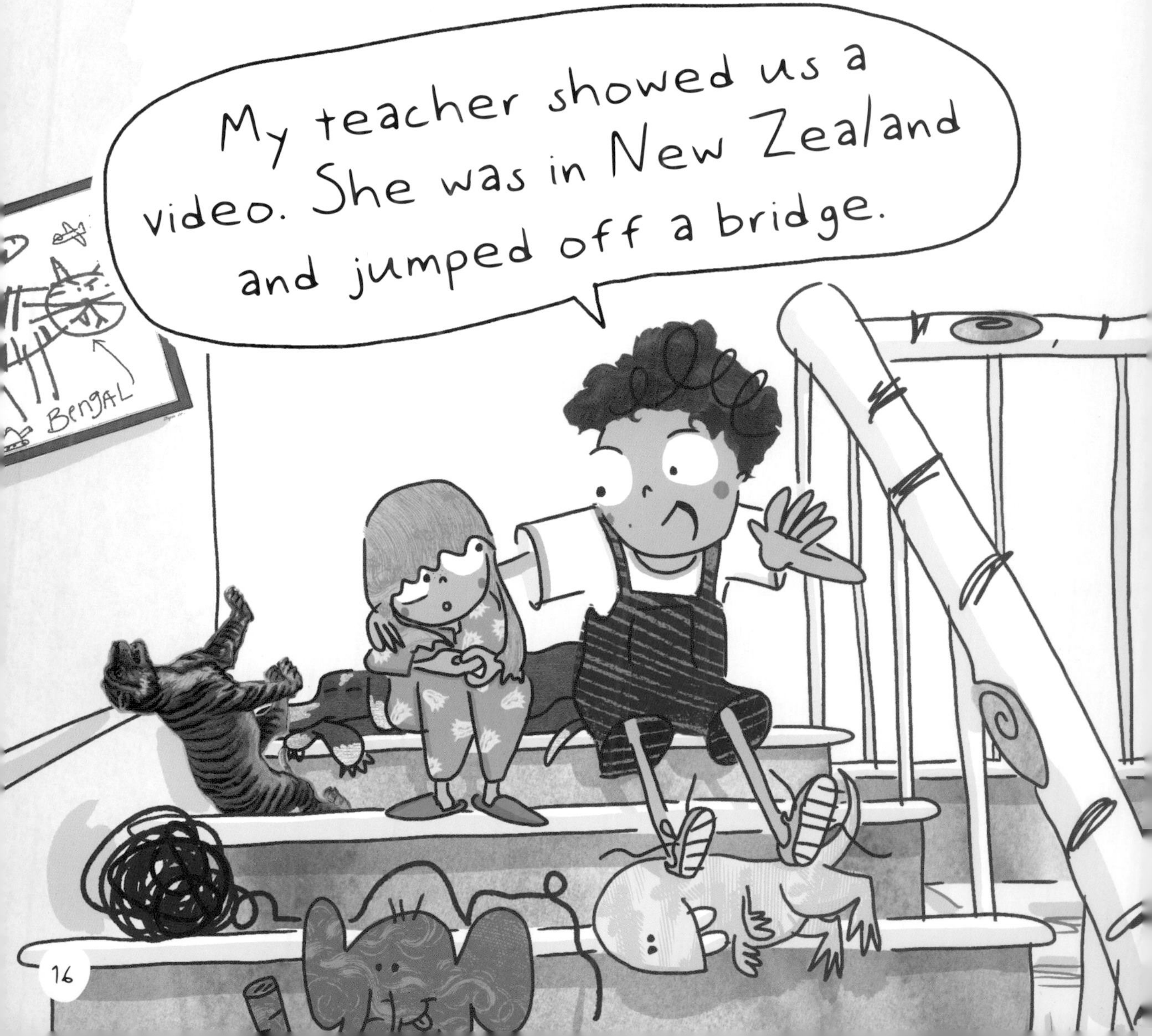

"What do you mean?" says my little sister.
She gets scared a lot.

"She tied a rope on her leg," I say. "She jumped
off, then she bounced around. It is called bungee
jumping. It is very cool."

"Ohhhhhhh."

We look at the stuffed animals.
And a big ball of yarn.
And the banister.
And we know exactly
what to do.

In my best TV sports voice, I say:

But when I pick up Bengal, my little sister says,
"Not Bengal."

"BENGAL IS READY TO JUMP!" I yell.

She says, "He wants to stay with me."

Before Bengal was hers, he was mine.
So how would she know anything?

I grab the ball of yarn.

"He doesn't like jumping!" says my little sister.

I tie one end of the yarn to Bengal's leg.

"He hates jumping and he hates this game!" says
my little sister.

She is wrong.

11:33 AM
CHAPTER 4½
TIME OUT

My big brother is across the street with his friend.

My little sister is taking a nap.

My dad is reading.

I am drawing.

"How about you and me walk to the library?"
asks Mom.

"Yes!"

I love getting books from the library.

"I thought you might like a breather," says Mom.

"What is a breather?" I ask.

"A breather is like a time-out that you want
to take."

The walk to the library has one hill.

When we walk with my little sister, it takes forever.
When I walk with Mom, it takes no time.

I can walk really fast.

We get to the library, my favorite place.

"You can check out as many books as you can hold on the walk home. Go nuts!"

My mom is whispering.

"Remember: Go nuts, quietly. This is the library."

Mom knows I can be
a little loud.

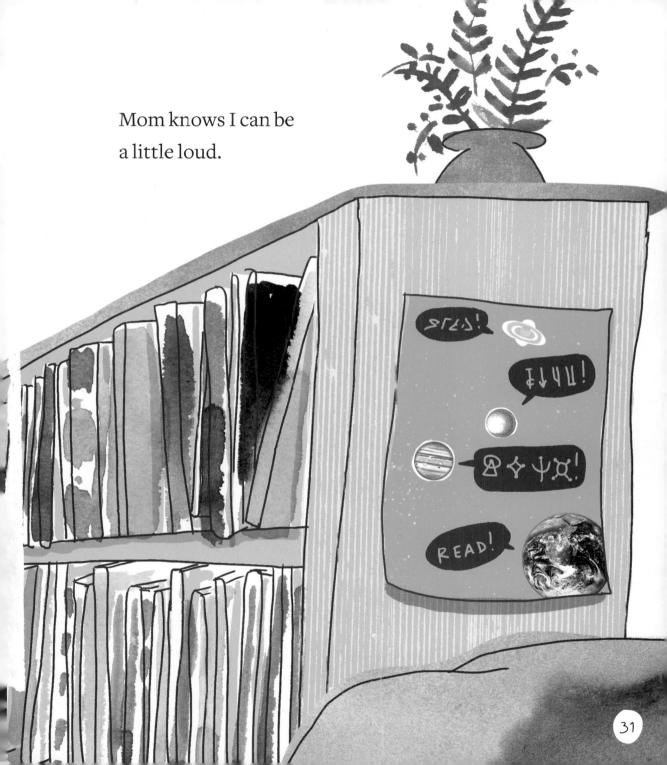

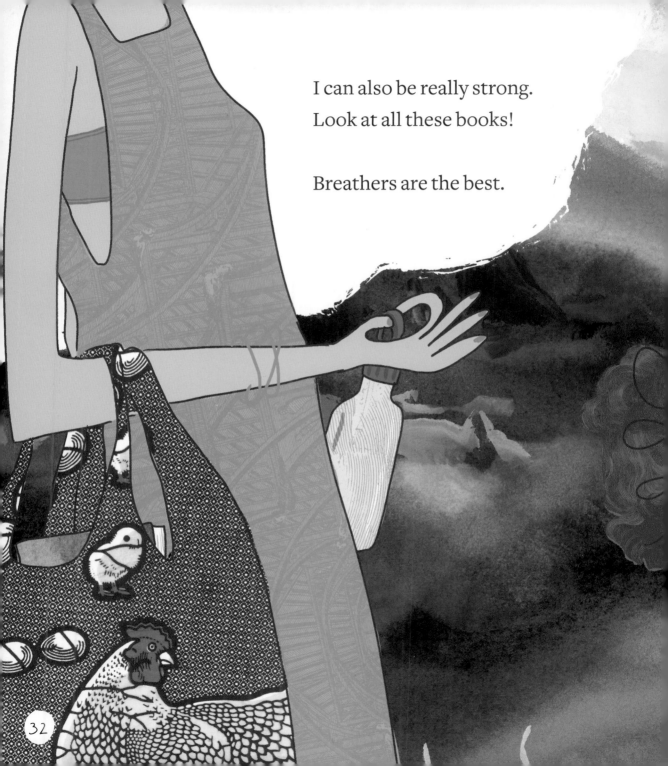

I can also be really strong.
Look at all these books!

Breathers are the best.

32

THE BEST CASTLE DRAWINGS
TREEHOUSE RESEARCH
SO MANY DOGS
STINKY!
THE PLAN-PLANET
MAPS
HE HAS BAD DAYS LIKE ME
HOME!

3:15 PM

CHAPTER 6
THE SECRET

There are lots of woods around our house.
Today we are exploring where none of us have ever
been before.

It's one of our favorite things to do.

We get to some big trees that fell over. There is only one way through.

"Move over, you two," says my big brother. "Only a boss can figure this out."

But he is too tall.
He does not fit.

"Tigers can crawl through anything,"
says my little sister.

But she is too short. She cannot climb.

"My turn!" I say.
I am the perfect size.

Wow.

I cannot wait to draw all of this.

"So what's behind the trees?" asks my big brother.

"Anything for a tiger to eat?" asks my little sister.

"Tell us!" they say.

I think for a second.

"Nothing you guys would like," I lie.

This is my secret.

We got popsicles!

Everything is great.

And then a bee shows up.

Mom shoos it away. Her hand hits my big brother.

OH NO!

The top half of his popsicle goes flying.

"My bad," says my mom. She hands him
a new one.

The bee comes back.

My little sister has that look like she is about
to cry A LOT.

We are all afraid of that look.

My dad runs over with the box of popsicles.

"Hey, tough cookie!" he says. "Have another one."

Finally, the bee flies away.

That is when I do some math.

Not Fair

Big brother → DUH.

$$1 + \frac{1}{2} = 1\frac{1}{2}$$

47

My mom and dad look in the box.

Then they look at me.

The box is empty.

48

7:09 PM
CHAPTER 8
ALONE

I am in the basement. Alone. Finally.

I am drawing the tree house from the woods.

At first, I draw what I remember. Then I add what I want in my own tree house.

I really like that part of drawing.

52

I can hear my big brother and little sister standing at the top of the stairs.

I don't look at them. I am taking a breather.

I guess they do not know about breathers.

"How do you come up with this stuff?" says my big brother.

"Draw me a tree house!"
says my little sister.

I put down the crayons.

I have an idea.

They are running around
doing exactly what I say.

And I am right in the middle.

Sometimes that is the best
place to be.

8:48 PM
CHAPTER 9
GOOD NIGHT
Sniffle.
Sniffle, sniffle-waaaaaaa . . .
SNORE.
Sniffle-sniffle.
Waaaaaaaaaaaaaaaaaaaaaaa-waaaaaaaaaaaaaaaaaaaaaaa-WAAAAAAAAAAAAAA!!!!!
Zzzzz

Then they say nothing.

It is finally quiet.

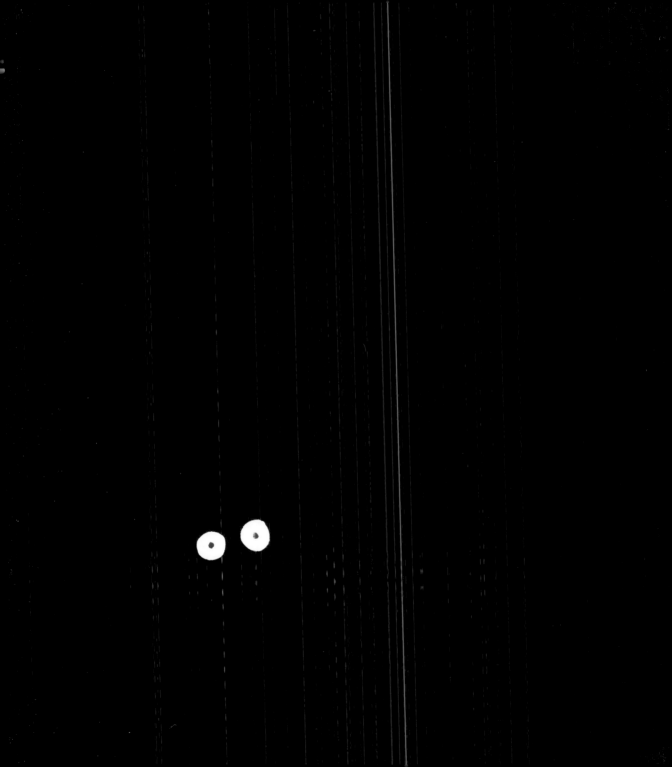

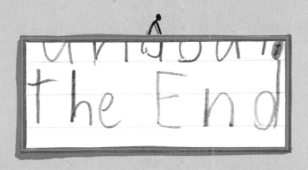
the End

Keep out

CLASS PROGRAM

Date | | | | |

	Family Name			Given Name			Class		Room	
	MON.	RM.	TUES.	RM.	WED.	RM.	THURS.	RM.	FRI.	RM.
1										
2										
3										
4										
5										
6										
7										
8										
9										
10										
11										
12										

NAME_____**ADDRESS**_____